T0145199

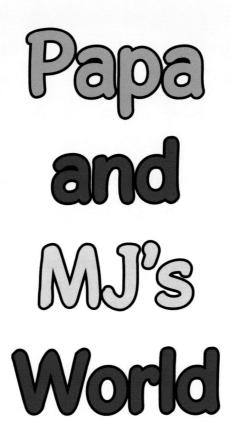

Papa and MJ's World

By: Dr. Katrena Robinson, Ph.D. & D. Min.

Copyright © 2022 by Dr. Katrena Robinson, Ph.D. & D. Min.. 818027

All rights reserved. No part of this book may be reproduced or transmitted in any form or by any means, electronic or mechanical, including photocopying, recording, or by any information storage and retrieval system, without permission in writing from the copyright owner.

This is a work of fiction. Names, characters, places and incidents either are the product of the author's imagination or are used fictitiously, and any resemblance to any actual persons, living or dead, events, or locales is entirely coincidental.

To order additional copies of this book, contact:
Xlibris
844-714-8691
www.Xlibris.com
Orders@Xlibris.com

ISBN: Softcover   978-1-6698-0537-3
Hardcover   978-1-6698-0538-0
EBook   978-1-6698-0536-6

Print information available on the last page

Rev. date: 01/17/2022

Papa
and
MJ's
World

Dedication

This book is dedicated to the author's husband, Carlton Robinson, Sr. and his relationship that he has with his first grandson, Marcus Shaw, Jr. affectionately called MJ. After having granddaughters, he is so proud and blessed to have a grandson who calls him Papa. Their relationship blossomed into a special bond from when he first saw MJ. It was love at first sight, and the feeling was mutual.

He also babysits MJ daily and enjoys every minute of it. Papa and MJ have a bond that cannot be broken. They seal their special bond each time when they see each other with their special fist bump. It does not matter whether grandsons call their, grandfather, Papa, Grandpa, Opa, Gdad, Gramps, Big Paw, Grandpappy, Granddad Grandaddy, Big Daddy, Gpaw, Pop, Grampa, or Peepaw, it is universal that grandfathers send a message to their grandsons that say, "I love you, and I am proud to be your grandfather."

MJ's mom pulls up in the driveway. She unbuckles MJ's car seat and takes him out of the car. She rushes in the front door. MJ jumps out of his mom's arms and into his Papa's arms. He looks at Papa and jumps up and down. He knows it is about to be on and popping.

MJ and Papa give each other their special fist bump. He waves bye-bye to his mom. MJ's says, "Papa, it is just you and me!" He gives Papa a sneaky smile. MJ knows that he has enter into Papa and MJ's world.

MJ is so happy. He gets to spend the day with Papa. MJ lays on Papa's shoulder. Papa's heart beats with love. Papa hugs MJ and say, "My only and favorite grandson. You're my boy! I love you so much! Look around the house. It is all yours. You are in Papa and MJ's World!"

"My only and favorite grandson."

MJ points to the kitchen. He says, "Papa, I am hungry". Papa opens the refrigerator. MJ points to the bacon. He says, "I want bacon." Papa says, "You can eat whatever you want to eat. It's just you and me. You are in Papa and MJ's World."

MJ climbs up on the bar stool and sits in it. Papa gives him his bacon along with his favorite juice. Papa and MJ sit at the bar and eat their breakfast. Papa, says, "Is it good?" MJ smiles and says, "Yah." MJ knows that food tastes better in Papa and MJ's world.

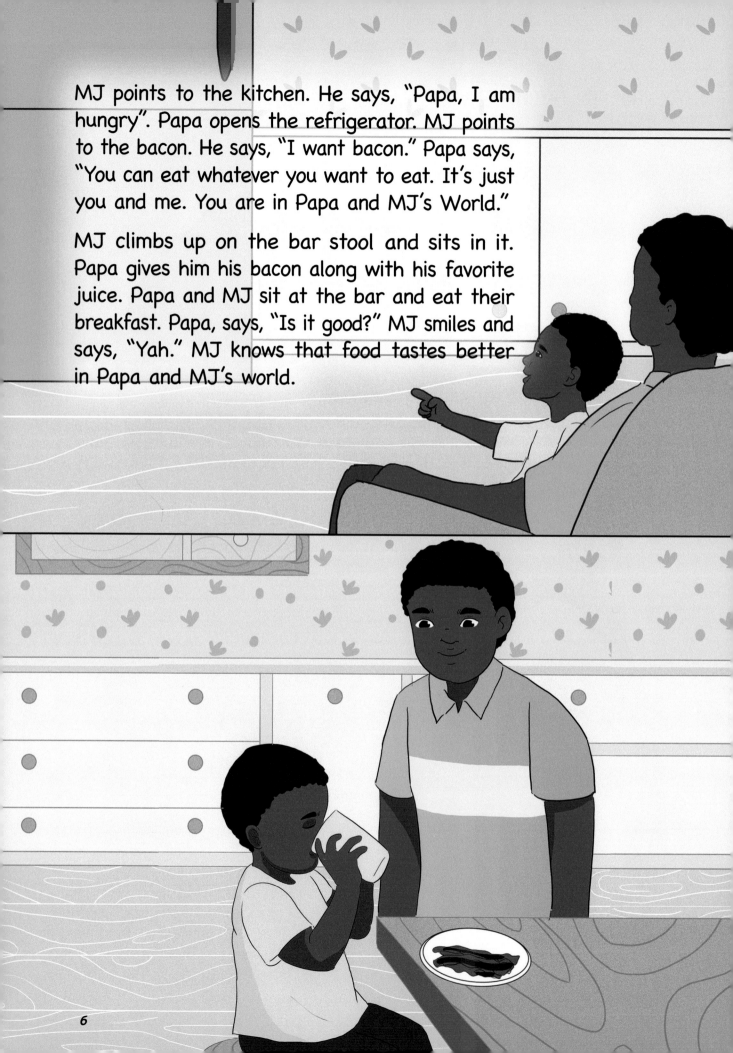

After breakfast, Papa lays back in his recliner. MJ lays back in his recliner next to Papa. MJ says, "Papa, I want to watch my favorite movie." Papa knows that means he can't watch his western movie. Papa knows that MJ controls the tv. MJ can watch whatever he wants to watch on tv. He's in Papa and MJ's world.

After watching his favorite movie, they play the name game. Papa says, "What your name?" MJ says, "Marcus Shaw!" Papa say, "What's your name?" MJ says, "Marcus Shaw!" MJ says his name with pride and laughter. He is named after his dad. MJ loves playing the name game with Papa. He is in Papa and MJ's World.

MJ runs to the toy chest. He pulls out all of his toys. Papa is getting sleepy now. MJ runs over and shakes Papa's leg to wake him up. He says, "Wake up Papa. Look at my fire truck." MJ pretends that he is driving his fire truck and is on the way to put out a fire. You can hear the loud siren on the fire truck. MJ will not let Papa go to sleep. Papa knows that he must stay awake. He is in Papa and MJ world.

Papa has to go to the office. He quietly removes MJ from his arms. He lays MJ down and covers him up with his favorite blanket. Uh-oh, Papa knows to be careful . MJ just might open that one eye to let him know…….. I see you. It is hard to sneak away from MJ in Papa and MJ's World.

Suddenly, Papa hears some tiny feet running to the door. MJ peeps inside the door. Papa says, "MJ, "you are supposed to be asleep." MJ looked up at Papa with those beautiful and sleepy eyes. Papa knew that MJ could not sleep. He has to be laying in Papa's arms. That's the way MJ sleeps in Papa and MJ's World.

Papa says, "It's lunchtime." MJ jumps up and down with joy. Papa says, "MJ, let's go and get in the car." MJ knows that he gets to take a ride. Papa puts MJ in his car seat and fasten his seatbelt. He backs out of the garage. Finally, Papa pulls up at "Burger World." MJ yells," It's cheese burger time! Cheese burger everyday only happens in Papa and MJ's World!"

After lunch, MJ is bursting with energy. He gets on his toy school bus. He is a bus driver. He rides up and down the hall. MJ rides from room to room pretending to pick up children at the bus stop. Papa shakes his head. He says, "MJ can be the best bus driver in Papa and MJ's world."

Papa says, "MJ, I can't keep up with you, but I will try." MJ asks, "Are you riding the school bus today?" Papa says, "I am going to miss the school bus today." MJ pulls off. Papa pretends to be running and trying to catch the school bus. Papa loves to have make believe fun with MJ. Papa knows that MJ is a fun school bus driver in Papa and MJ's World.

MJ runs down the hall. Papa hears a ball bouncing. He looks down the hall and sees MJ playing basketball. MJ dribbles the ball and throws it in the basket. Papa says, "There it is! Yes, two points MJ!" Look out professional basketball teams. MJ is coming for you! A basketball star is in the making! Nobody loves and can shoot a basketball like MJ in Papa and MJ's world."

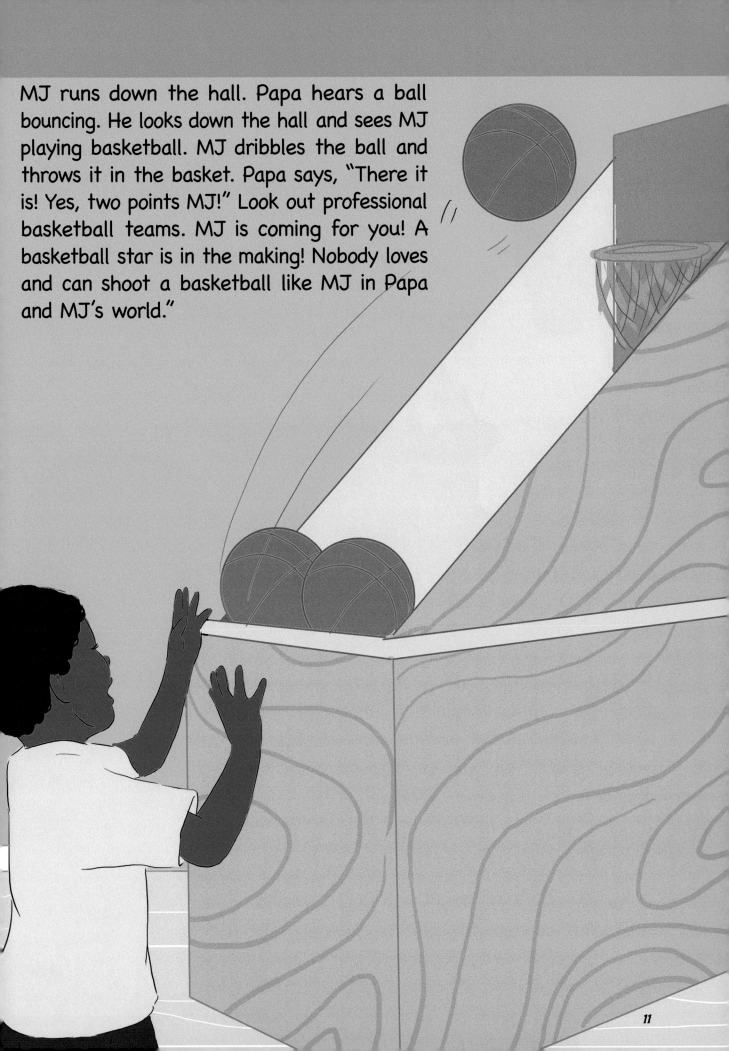

Papa says, "I am tired MJ. Let's sit down and rest." Papa sits down and falls asleep. MJ says, "Papa, look at me!" Papa quickly jumps and sits up. He sees MJ walking in his shoes. Papa says, "MJ, I am proud to see my grandson walking in my shoes." Papa says, "One day you will walk in my footsteps." This is a proud and special moment in Papa and MJ's World.

Papa says, "Now that I am up. Let's go fishing before your mom comes to take you home." Papa grabs their fishing pole, bucket, chairs and baits from the garage. They put on their fishing caps. Papa says, "This is the best gift ever to teach my four-year-old grandson how to fish. This can only happen in Papa and MJ's world."

They go outside and sit by the lake. Papa unfolds their chairs so they can sit down and relax. Papa sits in his chair. MJ sits in his mini chair right beside Papa. Papa puts a bait on his hook. MJ says, "Papa put a bait on my hook." Papa throws MJ's pole in the lake. He sits back down to wait on a fish to bite. Papa says, "What a wonderful world, just you and me in Papa and MJ's world."

All of a sudden, Papa sees a fish tugging at MJ's pole. Papa jumps up and let MJ helps reel it in. MJ begins screaming, "Papa I got one. It's a big fish!" Papa begins smiling and says, "MJ, you just caught your first fish. What a beauty! It is about the size of my hand." Papa takes the fish off the hook and puts it in the bucket. Papa says, "Let's call it a day and go inside. What an awesome day for fishing in Papa and MJ's world!"

When they get inside, Papa's alarm clock goes off. MJ knows what that means. His mom is coming to pick him up soon. He folds those little arms hoping Papa cuts that alarm clock off quickly. MJ keeps looking at the door. Suddenly, his mom bursts through the door. She says, "Hey MJ, did you enjoy Papa today?" MJ says, "Yes, I did! I love hanging out with Papa in Papa and MJ's world."

Then MJ looks at his mom. He is sad. His mom says, "It's time to go home". MJ screams, cries and hold on to Papa's leg tightly. Papa wipes his tears from MJ's eyes. Papa and MJ do their special fist bump. Papa says, "It's okay MJ, don't cry. Be a big boy! Tomorrow you will come back. We will have fun all over again in Papa and MJ's World."

Acknowledgements

I like to thank God for blessing my husband to experience the joy and great pride in having a grandson. I like to thank my grandson for being a handsome, sweet, smart, fun, and loving little boy, which makes it so easy for my husband to take care of him while his mom and dad go to work. I like to thank my son-in-law, Marcus Shaw, Sr. and my daughter, Chakea Robinson-Shaw for blessing us with our first grandson and for allowing my husband, who is affectionally called Papa to develop a special bond with our first grandson based on love, appreciation, fun and pure joy.